Music is NOT banned!

GirlFriendZ
Flash Mob to Go
by Roger Hurn
Illustrated by Kenny Kiernan

Published by Ransom Publishing Ltd.
Radley House, 8 St. Cross Road, Winchester, Hampshire
SO23 9HX, UK
www.ransom.co.uk

ISBN   978 178127 154 4
First published in 2013

Flash Mob
to Go

Roger Hurn

Illustrated by Kenny Kiernan

Ransom

Kelly Montez

Like · Comment · Friend

Hey, I'm Kelly Montez, and unless you've been living in a cave for the past year you'll know I'm in the band *GirlFriendZ*.

Yeah, that's right, I'm the one with the killer looks and a voice like gravel dipped in honey. And *GirlFriendZ* is the number one band in the world – or it *was*, until the day the aliens invaded Earth and banned music! Those creepoids are *so* not cool.

But don't worry guys, we're not going to let them get away with that. *GirlFriendZ* will carry on making music and there's no way a bunch of alien weirdos in MIB (Music is Banned) is going to stop us!

Yaz Jackson

Like · Comment · Friend

Hiya guys, Yaz here. I was born in a circus and my mum and dad were acrobats, so that's why I'm always doing somersaults, cartwheels and back flips on stage. On our next tour I'm gonna walk across the stage on a high wire! How cool is that?

Yeah, you did hear me right. There WILL be another *GirlFriendZ* tour – just as soon as we find a way to send the Zargons back to their home planet with their creepy alien tails between their legs.

Olivia Parsons

Like · Comment · Friend

Hi *GirlFriendZ* fans. My name is Olivia – but everyone calls me Liv. I know I look like the girl next door, but I can be a bit of a wild child when it comes to music! I just love getting up on stage and singing my heart out!

But now those freaky aliens are arresting musicians and destroying all the musical instruments they can get their tentacles on! It makes me so mad, but they'll never catch us and stop us singing.

That's a promise!

Eve Rossi

Like · Comment · Friend

Hello everybody. I'm Eve, the girl with the crazy hair and the personality to match!

It's great being in *GirlFriendZ* 'cos it gives me the chance to wear all kinds of amazing outfits. I love designing my own clothes and it gives me a buzz when I see you guys copying my look!

I know the Zargons are trying to stop us having fun – but don't fret guys, we are *so* gonna have the last laugh!

Charlotte Opirah

Like · Comment · Friend

OK, it's me, Charlotte. Usually I'd rather sing than talk, 'cos I'm the best singer in the band. Hey, just kidding!!

But I've got something to say that can't be put into a song. It's this. We absolutely *have* to find a way to beat the Zargons! They must have a weakness – and I've got a suspicion it has something to do with music.

Think about it guys. They have banned music and they're doing some kind of alien mind-wipe, so musicians and singers forget how to play and sing. Why? Well, I'm gonna make it my business to find out!

Finn the roadie

Like · Comment · Friend

Hey, I'm Finn and I have the best job in the world. I'm the *roadie* (that's road manager) for *GirlFriendZ*. Well, it *was* the best job until the Zargons arrived and we had to go on the run. Now my job is about getting the girls to their secret gigs *and* keeping them out of the Zargon's clutches! You see, the Zargon agents of MIB track down musicians and singers and take them off to the 'harmony' camps to have their minds wiped. Then, when they come out of the camps, they can't remember how to play or sing.

GirlFriendZ are the last band left, so MIB are desperate to catch them. If they do that, then that really *will* be the day music dies. But I'm never going to let that happen!

The Zargons

The Zargons are an alien race from the Andromeda galaxy. They have developed advanced technology that enables their starships to travel faster than the speed of light.

They are humanoid in appearance and, contrary to popular opinion, they do not possess tentacles (or tails!). However, in certain conditions, their eyes glow like cats' eyes.

They are on a mission to eradicate all forms of music from the universe. To this end, the Zargons build 'harmony' camps on the planets they invade. Anyone with musical talent is taken to the camps by Zargon agents of MIB (*Music Is Banned*), where they are subjected to a process known as 'mind wiping'. The mind-wipe has the effect of making the musician or singer forget how to play or sing. In street slang this process is known as 'soul stealing'.

The main feature of the 'harmony' camps are the giant incinerators where musical instruments are destroyed.

It is believed that the Zargons' hatred of music stems from the fact that music is the only thing that has the power to defeat them. (See article: *vampires*, *garlic*, *crosses*.)

Prologue

London, England. Saturday 2nd August 2025

'Thank you Wembley. It's been emotional.'

Kelly punched the air with her fist and 70,000 fans screamed back at her. Yaz, Olivia, Eve and Charlotte, the other members of *GirlFriendZ*, jumped up and down on the stage like hyperactive kangaroos. Waves of love washed over them from their fans. If they hadn't known they were the world's biggest band before this gig – they knew it now!

'Hey, listen to those guys,' yelled Charlotte.

'Yay, it's awesome,' Eve yelled back at her.

Olivia grinned like a cat with a bowl of double cream. 'It just doesn't get any better than this.'

'Yes it does,' said Yaz. 'This show's being beamed worldwide by satellite. Billions of people are going mad for us.'

* * * * * * *

Suddenly a huge shadow covered the stadium. The howling crowd fell silent. A giant starship hovered over Wembley.

At first people thought it was part of the show. But then a red laser light shot out from the ship and vapourised the Wembley

arch. A metallic voice rang out into the stunned silence.

'People of Earth, go to your homes and stay there. This is an order. Failure to obey will be punishable by death. This planet is now a province of the Zargon Empire.'

One
Captured!

Kelly, Eve, Charlotte, Yaz and Liv clung onto each other for dear life as Finn, their road manager, drove the battered old van like a maniac in his efforts to shake off the jet-powered MIB cruiser in hot pursuit of them.

'We'll never outrun them in this bone-shaker,' yelled Kelly.

'Yes, do something, Finn!' howled Charlotte.

Finn ground his teeth. 'I'm doing my best,' he muttered.

'Well, that may not be enough,' screamed Eve, as the cruiser pulled alongside them and forced them off the road.

Finn jumped out of the van, yelling at the girls to run for their lives. He raced off into the woods.

But, before the girls could follow him, the grim-faced Zargon agents leapt out of their vehicle and sprinted over to the van.

'Don't worry guys,' said Kelly. 'We'll sing at them. Zargons can't cope with music, it makes their brains go funny.'

The world's most famous group had never felt less like singing, but they knew it was their only chance. But, as the girls opened their mouths to hit the Zargons with the full force of *Back Beat, Street Beat*, one of their world-wide hits, the MIB squad pulled out ear defenders and put them on.

An MIB officer strode up to them. 'Sing away, *GirlFriendZ*,' she snarled. 'We can't hear you.'

The agents grabbed the girls.

'But *you* can hear me, I think,' the MIB officer continued. 'And I'm saying you are going to be taken to the 'harmony' camps, where you will have your minds wiped.' She smiled nastily. 'And then you will *never* sing again!'

Two

Doomed!

The MIB agents bundled the girls into the back of a transporter and whisked them off under armed guard to the nearest 'harmony' camp.

GirlFriendZ had been performing a gig at a secret location when the MIB agents had suddenly arrived to stop the show and arrest the girls. They were still wearing their stage costumes. They looked like brightly coloured birds of paradise caged up inside the dark and gloomy vehicle.

'Do you think Finn escaped?' asked Liv.

'Probably,' said Eve. 'He's a fast runner.'

'Huh!' said Charlotte sourly. 'Pity he isn't a fast driver. If he was, then maybe MIB wouldn't have caught us!'

'MIB don't care about his running abilities,' said Kelly bitterly. 'So they won't waste their energy chasing him. They're only after people who can sing and play instruments – like us!'

'And Finn can't sing a note or play any instrument – but he's a smart guy,' said Yaz. 'He'll find a way to help us.'

Yaz always looked on the bright side of things. Charlotte didn't. She folded her arms and slumped back against the side of the transporter. 'Well, I hope you're right, Yaz, 'cos if he doesn't, the soul-stealing Zargon freaks will mind-wipe us – and then we're doomed!'

Three

Finn Calling

Kelly, Liv, Eve, Yaz and Charlotte stood outside the barracks where they were being kept until the Zargons were ready to mind-wipe them. MIB guards patrolled the wire fence of the 'harmony' camp, making escape impossible.

However, the girls were not the only prisoners in the camp. MIB agents had also captured all the members of the

world-famous City Symphony Orchestra. Sir Ozwald Shaker, the orchestra's conductor, came over to talk to them.

'I see MIB has caught you too,' he said. 'I fear they plan to mind-wipe us all tomorrow.' He glanced over at the guards. 'And there is *nothing* we can do to stop them.'

Kelly shook her head. 'No, we've tried singing at them but, because of those ear defenders they wear, they can't hear us.'

Sir Ozwald looked thoughtful. 'If we only had our instruments, we could play so loudly that their ear defenders would be unable to block out our music.' He sighed. 'But when they arrested us, they also took our instruments away.'

Then Sir Ozwald pointed to the tall chimney that towered over the camp. 'The camp leaders have already taken great delight in telling us that a lorry is bringing our beloved instruments here and that we will be forced to watch the Zargons throw them into the flames of the incinerator before they mind-wipe us.'

Just then a ringtone of *HotshotZ*, one of *GirlFriendZ*' big hits, came from Eve's silver boots. Quickly she reached down and pulled out a smartphone from a hidden compartment in the heel. She grinned at the astonished conductor.

'I design all my own clothes,' she said. 'And a girl can never have too many secret pockets!'

She looked at the screen and Finn's face grinned back at her. *'Kelly was right,'* she thought. *'The Zargons haven't caught him.'*

'Hey', he said. 'I've a plan to bust you girls out of that camp, but we're going to need a flash mob to do it.'

Eve frowned. 'That's cool,' she said. 'But where on Earth are we going to get a flash mob from?'

'That's not a problem,' Finn replied. 'You've got the flash mob right there with you!'

Four

Truck Stop

The MIB container lorry pulled into the motorway service station car park. It was filled with confiscated musical instruments. The lorry was taking them to the camp to be destroyed in the giant incinerators. The driver and the guard climbed down from the cab.

'Shouldn't one of us stay with the lorry?' said the guard.

The driver shook his head. 'We need some food, and anyway no human would be foolish enough to steal an MIB truck.

They are far too scared of being taken to the 'harmony' camps.'

The guard nodded. 'We should mind-wipe all humans, and not just the musicians and singers,' he growled. 'Then we'd rid them of their disgusting love of music for good.'

The driver scowled. 'I couldn't agree more. Humans and their *music* make my skin crawl!'

The guard clapped him on the shoulder. 'Don't worry, my friend,' he said. 'MIB is winning the war and now we've caught *GirlFriendZ and* the City Symphony Orchestra, we are well on the way to wiping music off the face of this world forever.'

Finn appeared from behind the truck. He held a smartphone in his hand. 'Well, let's see about that, shall we guys?' he said. As the startled Zargons fumbled with their

ear defenders, he hit them with a blast of
HotshotZ and they crumpled to the ground.

Finn dragged their unconscious bodies
behind some wheelie bins. Then, wearing
the MIB driver's cap and jacket, he
clambered up into the lorry's cab and drove
off in the direction of the camp.

Five

An Orchestrated Escape

Finn held up his stolen ID and the MIB guards on the gate waved him through without a second glance. He drove into the loading area just by the incinerator. He hit Eve's number on speed dial. When she answered he said, 'OK Eve, flash mob to go!'

Eve snapped her phone shut. 'Let's go, guys,' she yelled. 'We've got a gig to play.'

To the amazement of the MIB guards, Kelly, Charlotte, Yaz, Liv, Eve and the whole City Symphony Orchestra suddenly raced over to the lorry. Finn flung the doors open and the musicians frantically grabbed their instruments.

Immediately, the MIB guards realised what was happening. An MIB officer barked an order at them, but they couldn't hear her because they were all wearing ear defenders. The officer pulled hers from her head and gestured at the guards to do the same. Then she pointed at the orchestra. 'Stop them!' she screamed. The guards nodded and charged.

They were closing fast.

Sir Ozwald turned to Kelly. His face was drained and pale. 'It's no good, he said. 'We don't have time to tune up.'

Kelly shrugged. 'Don't worry about it, Ozzie, the Zargons won't know the difference. Now hit it!'

Sir Ozwald waved his baton and the orchestra launched into the opening chords of *HotshotZ*. The sound waves hit the

Zargons with all the majestic power of a
musical tsunami. The MIB guards
collapsed, rolling and writhing helplessly
on the ground before they burst into
flames!

'Quick, everybody, get in the lorry,'
yelled Finn. 'We're out of here!'

The girls, Sir Ozwald and the orchestra
piled into the back of the truck and made
their escape.

* * * * * * *

Later that night, an MIB patrol cruiser found the empty lorry abandoned in a lay-by miles from the camp. There was no sign of *GirlFriendZ* or the City Symphony Orchestra.

To the fury of the Zargons, *GirlFriendZ* had once again survived to continue their mission to keep music alive.

Will the Zargons ever defeat GirlFriendZ ?